Dog Goes to Nursery School

by LUCILLE HAMMOND
illustrated by EUGENIE

A GOLDEN BOOK, New York
Western Publishing Company, Inc., Racine, Wisconsin 53404

Text copyright © 1982 by Western Publishing Company, Inc. Illustrations copyright © 1982 by Eugenie Fernandes. All rights reserved. Printed in the U.S.A. No part of this book may be reproduced or copied in any form without written permission from the publisher. GOLDEN®, GOLDEN® & DESIGN, A FIRST LITTLE GOLDEN BOOK®, and A GOLDEN BOOK® are trademarks of Western Publishing Company, Inc. Library of Congress Catalog Card Number: 81-86493 ISBN 0-307-10134-7/ ISBN 0-307-68134-3 (lib. bdg.)   E F G H I J

ONE morning Dog's mother woke him up early. "Today is a special day," she said. "Today is the first day of nursery school."

Dog was glad that it was a special day. But he was not so glad about school. At school he might miss his mother. At school he might miss his favorite toys.

So Dog said, "I don't want to go to school. I want to stay home with you."
But Dog's mother told him that he was a big dog now, and that big dogs go to school.

Dog washed his hands and face and brushed his teeth. He hoped his mother would forget about school.

"Today I am going to make a picture with my crayons," he said.

"No," said his mother. "Today you are going to school."

Dog got dressed. He brought his blocks into the kitchen. "Today," said Dog, "I am going to build a castle with my blocks."

"No," said his mother. "Today you are going to school."

Then Dog ate his breakfast. He said to his
mother, "Today I am going to play with my
little red car."

"No," said his mother. "Today you are
going to school."

So Dog and his mother went to school.

There were many other dogs at school. All the chairs and tables were just the right size for dogs.

There were toys and games
that dogs like to play with.

There was a special place to look at books and a special place to paint. On the walls hung pictures that dogs had made.

In one corner Dog saw a playhouse with real furniture and real dishes. The dogs in the playhouse were dressed up in hats and funny clothes. They were pretending to be grownups.

On the floor two dogs had built a long track for a train. Each dog had a little train and sometimes they bumped their trains together. The dogs were laughing.

Dog's mother kissed him good-by
and left him with the teacher. Dog
began to cry.

The teacher asked Dog if he would like to make a picture with some crayons.

"Yes," whispered Dog, and he made a picture with the crayons.

After that the teacher asked him if he would like to build a castle with some blocks.

"Yes," said Dog, and he built a castle with the blocks.

Then the teacher asked him if he would like to play with a little red car.

"Yes!" said Dog, and for a long time he played with the little red car.

When it was time to go home, Dog said good-by to his teacher. Dog's mother was waiting for him outside the door. He gave her a big hug.

"Today," said Dog, "I made a picture with some crayons. And today," he said, "I built a castle with some blocks. And today I played with a little red car."

"Yes," said his mother. "And today you went to school!"